Tom,

I'm sure you and Alfie will enjoy
exploring Long Ashton on bikes too.

Charlotte Ratcliffe

Matilda and the Magic Bike

Limited Special Edition. No. 25 of 25 Paperbacks

The magic starts with you.

Charlotte joined the army at age 16 and a half as an army chef. She served 15 years in the army and received four medals. Charlotte left the army to pursue her life-long dreams. She currently lives in Bristol doing what she loves, putting her imagination onto paper for everybody to enjoy.

CHARLOTTE RATCLIFFE

Matilda
and the
Magic Bike

AUSTIN MACAULEY PUBLISHERS™

LONDON • CAMBRIDGE • NEW YORK • SHARJAH

Copyright © Charlotte Ratcliffe (2019)

A CIP catalogue record for this title is available from the British Library.

ISBN 9781788489393 (Paperback)
ISBN 9781788489409 (Hardback)
ISBN 9781788489416 (E-Book)
www.austinmacauley.com

First Published (2019)
Austin Macauley Publishers Ltd
25 Canada Square
Canary Wharf
London
E14 5LQ

A huge thank you to the whole team at Austin Macauley Publishers for making my dream come true and for all your hard work and effort in publishing my book.

Dedicated to Charlotte Lloyd

I can't believe it's raining again, Matilda thought as she looked out of her grandmother's cottage window, her nose squashed against the glass. *Nothing ever happens here. It's so boring, the only exciting thing that has ever happened in the village was when Mrs Bumble thought her dog Popcorn had been dognapped because he'd been missing all day.* On this day, the whole village went out looking for Popcorn. Matilda remembered that they had looked everywhere, then PC Bloom heard muffled barks coming out of a rabbit hole, Popcorn had got stuck chasing rabbits. PC Bloom and two others had to dig Popcorn out. It had taken ages. Then the big missing dog case was closed.

It's days like this, I miss Mum and Dad, thought Matilda, looking at the wooden photo frame by her bed of all three of them eating a picnic at the beach. She then turned her head back to look at the heavy rain. Dad loved the rain, he always said that when it rains you should always plant a tree or a flower for good luck. 'The more the tree or flower grows, the more luck you will have in the future,' he said. Matilda and her mum and dad planted so many beautiful trees and flowers in the rain in their garden back in Bristol. It was like a magical garden, with many different flowers and trees, with bees and birds and all different kinds of insects, it was so beautiful. Matilda remembered once it was raining so heavily and they had just finished planting an apple tree. She, her mum and her dad slipped in the mud and could not get up for ages as they were laughing so much. *We were covered head-to-toe in mud. We looked like mud monsters,* laughed Matilda to herself.

I wish they would come home...

Matilda's parents were natural scientists, this meant they would go looking for natural plants, herbs, tree bark, and berries to heal people. Her dad believed that there was always a natural cure for everything, and that people just had to find it. He had told her once that in Willow tree bark, there is natural aspirin. This was interesting to Matilda. She loved listening to her dad and mum telling her of herbal remedies that they used in Ancient Greek and Egyptian times.

Her father Malcom Marsh and her mother Marie Marsh were the best natural scientists in the United Kingdom. Matilda's dad had got a letter three years ago, saying that some locals from the Amazon rainforest had found an unusual plant that could heal any illness. They needed Malcom and Marie's expert advice straight away, so Matilda's parents packed their brown leather suitcases, said goodbye, and said they would be back in two weeks—that was three years ago.

The science academy had told Matilda and her grandma that they lost contact with her parents. They had sent local tribes to look for them but no one could find them. "They must have come off the trail and gotten lost in the Amazon," said Mr Smith, the Head of the Academy. "The Amazon is a very big place, with many dangers," he said, but he also said that they would continue to look for them.

I know in my heart that they are still alive, and that one day they will come home to us, Matilda thought. 'If you believe hard enough and long enough, your dreams and wishes come true,' that's what Matilda's mum had told her.

"Matilda, dear," yelled her grandma, making Matilda jump.

"Yes, Grandma."

"I am going to the village shops to get some flour and eggs to make a cake. Would you like to come with me dear?"

"Well, I am bored. Yes, Grandma."

"OK dear, put your red raincoat on, it's raining cats and dogs out there today."

Raining cats and dogs, thought Matilda, *imagine if it did rain cats and dogs, you would have to have a strong umbrella that's for sure,'* giggled Matilda to herself. Matilda ran down the stairs, grabbed her red rain coat, put it on, and then her shoes, and waited by the door. Her grandma was in the hallway, singing at the top of her voice while looking ahead in the mirror in order to fix her hat.

Matilda loved her grandma and loved baking cakes with her. Matilda's favourite cake to bake was carrot cake, and her grandma's favourite was ginger cake. It was simple but very tasty, her grandma would say. Matilda's grandma was a small and round lady with big arms who gave the best cuddles. She had faded red hair and always wore her hair in a bun. Whenever she went out she always wore a hat. Matilda had asked her grandma why she always wore a hat. Her grandma had replied, "Got a head, get a hat." Matilda was unsure what this meant but that was what her grandma said. She also loved to sing anytime and anywhere, she said it was good for the soul.

"Right, Matilda, I am ready dear. Let me grab the umbrella and we are off."

Matilda and her grandma arrived at the village shop door, Matilda opened the old wooden door and as she opened it, the bell twinkled. Mr Dudley looked up and waved.

"Hello, Mrs Marsh, and hello Matilda, how are you today?"

"We are very well, thank you, Mr Dudley."

"Pardon?" said Mr Dudley.

"We are very well, thank you," said Matilda's grandma, a little louder this time.

"Pardon, Mrs Marsh? Can you speak louder please?"

Matilda noticed that Mr Dudley's hearing aid was on the counter. Matilda pointed at it. Mr Dudley looked down.

"Ahh, that's where it has gone, I have been looking for that all morning, Thank you Matilda." Mr Dudley picked it up and placed it in his ear. "Ahh that's better. Now, Mrs Marsh what did you say?"

"Never mind, dear."

"Right, well, what can I do for you today, Mrs Marsh?"

Matilda's grandma handed a list to Mr Dudley. Mr Dudley looked at it and scratched his head.

"Aww, baking them lovely cakes again, Mrs Marsh?"

"Indeed, Mr Dudley, I am."

"Right, now where did I put my glasses?"

Matilda started laughing.

"They're on top of your head, Mr Dudley."

Matilda often thought how Mr Dudley couldn't find anything. He was always losing something or misplacing an object here or there.

Mr Dudley was a funny-looking man with his wild white hair, and his bright red button nose that matched his bright red cheeks. *He always wore a dickie bow, a big baggy green cardigan with holes in it and funny round glasses with thick lenses, that looked like upside down jam jars,* chuckled Matilda to herself. But, Mr Dudley was the kindest man she had ever met, he would go above and beyond for anyone and helped everyone he could. He always gave Matilda a lollipop or chocolate bar whenever she visited him.

"Matilda, dear," yelled her grandma.

Matilda jumped out of her daydreaming.

"Yes, Grandma?"

"Right, I have just seen Mrs Bumble walk in to the post office and I wanted to have a quick word with her, so I won't be a minute, OK dear."

"OK Grandma."

Her grandma walked out of the shop door and the bell twinkled again.

Won't be a minute, laughed Matilda to herself, *more like three hours.* When her grandma and Mrs Bumble started talking, well, gossiping, they could spend hours talking about everything and everyone. Matilda's grandma wrote for the Long Ashton newsletter, so in a way it was her grandma's job to gossip and find everything out. Matilda walked over to a dusty wooden chair in the corner of the shop and sat down. It creaked as she sat on it. *I hope it doesn't break, thought Matilda nervously.*

"What's up Matilda? You don't look like your normal smiling self today?"

"I am just so bored, Mr Dudley. All my friends have gone to summer camps or gone on holidays and, well, I can't afford to go, so I have to stay in Long Ashton."

"Bored, hey. Well let me think, what I can do to turn that frown around," said Mr Dudley, tapping his chin. "Hmm, I have it," shouted Mr Dudley. "Why don't you help me?"

"What would I have to do?" asked Matilda.

"Well, it's a big job. Are you sure?"

"Yes."

"Well there is a cellar under the shop and it's full of junk and I have been meaning to clean it out for ages, and Mrs Dudley is always moaning at me to sort it out, but I haven't the time now, as Mrs Dudley has broken her ankle."

"Broken her ankle how, Mr Dudley?"

"Well, she fell over ice-skating last Saturday with her nieces and nephews. She will be fine Matilda, she just needs to rest it. So, you see, you would be doing me and Mrs Dudley a massive favour. I would pay you, of course."

"You don't have to Mr Dudley, I don't mind."

"Nonsense, hard work deserves rewards Matilda. How about five pounds a day?"

"Wow, that's great," smiled Matilda.

"I will have to ask your grandma first though."

At that moment, the shop door opened and Matilda's grandma walked in humming to herself.

"Are my ingredients ready, Mr Dudley?"

"Oh, yes, right Mrs Marsh, here you go." Mr Dudley placed a brown paper bag on the counter.

"Right dear, how much do I owe you?"

"Hmm, that will be £10.00 please, Mrs Marsh."

She looked in her handbag and pulled out her brown purse, opened it and gave Mr Dudley £10.00 pounds.

"Grandma."

"Yes, Matilda."

"Well, me and Mr Dudley were talking, and you know that I have been bored."

"Yes dear."

"Well, Mr Dudley has offered me a job."

Mr Dudley suddenly coughed.

"Well, if that's alright with you, Mrs Marsh."

"Well, of course is it," smiled Matilda's grandma. "What do I always say, Matilda? If you can't find an adventure, make one."

"What time would you like to start, Matilda?"

"Ermm, 9.00 am Mrs Marsh, please."

"9.00 am. The early bird catches the worm," smiled Matilda's grandma.

"Yippee!" shouted Matilda, skipping about the shop.

At that moment the shop bell went again, Matilda looked at the door. Oh no, thought Matilda. As she looked up Jessie, Jane, and Jenny walked in. Jane, the leader, looked up from her iPhone at Matilda.

"Well, well, well, Matilda Marsh."

"Found your parents yet?" laughed Jane.

"No," snapped Matilda.

"Maybe they just don't want to come back to you," said Jessie.

"Or maybe they are having such a good time without you that they don't want to come back," laughed Jenny.

At that moment Matilda's grandma came over.

"Hello girls."

"Hello Mrs Marsh," Jane, Jessie and Jenny said together.

"Right, Matilda, we have to make a move now."

"OK," said Matilda. "Bye, Mr Dudley.

"See you tomorrow, Matilda."

"Bye Matilda," said Jane.

Matilda just stared at Jane, going red in the cheeks with anger.

"Matilda, don't be rude, say goodbye to Jane."

Matilda said a quick goodbye and walked out the door. As she walked outside, she could hear Jane, Jessie and Jenny laughing very loudly, As Matilda walked home, she thought about how she could never understand why Jane, Jessie and Jenny were always so mean to her. Even on her first day at nursery, Matilda was playing with a doll and Jane came over and snatched the doll and hit Matilda with it. From that day on things had not got any better with Jane, Jessie and Jenny. Matilda was still feeling really upset about what the girls had said, then she remembered what her mum had told her once, 'Holding onto anger is like grasping a hot coal with the intent of throwing it at someone else, you are the one who gets burned'. Suddenly, she felt all the anger go, she carried on walking alongside her grandma.

Matilda suddenly heard a ringing sound in her ears. She sleepily opened one eye, then looked at the clock. She yawned, then reached her thin pale arm and slapped the alarm clock off. She then opened the other eye, stretched, and threw her quilt off herself and jumped out of bed. *Burr, it's freezing,* Matilda thought. She walked over to her bedroom window, wiped away the condensation on the glass with her hand and stared out of the window. She could hear the wind whistling through the trees, and she could see the leaves blowing around in circles. She hugged herself, *Better put something warm on today.* Suddenly, Matilda's grandma burst through the door, singing at the top of her voice.

"Ohh, whhaaat aaa bbbeeauutiful mmmorning, ooh what a beautiful day."

Matilda nearly jumped ten feet off the floor.

"Oh, you are up dear, just checking. Don't want you to be late on your first working day. Us Marsh girls are always on time. Now, wash up dear, and I will get your breakfast ready. Matilda's grandma then turned around on her heel and marched off and started singing again.

Matilda stared after her, blinking, *Well that woke me up,* thought Matilda.

After Matilda had washed she pulled on a heavy woolly jumper over her head. She looked in the mirror at her reflection. She was quite tall for her age, which was ten, she had long red hair, lots of freckles and bright green eyes. Her grandmother said that with every year she looked more like her father, with her green eyes and fiery red hair. She would catch her grandma on occasions looking at the family photos, crying. She knew that her grandma really missed her parents as much as Matilda did. *I know they're still alive. I know it.*

"Matilda," shouted her grandma, "Breakfast is on the table, quick, before it gets cold."

Matilda put her blue jeans on, socks, and combed her hair. She walked into the kitchen, which was always warm and cosy, she walked over to the big wooden table, pulled the chair out and sat down. In front of her was a big bowl of steaming hot porridge, with a chopped up banana in it. *Hmm, that smells so good,* thought Matilda. She picked up her spoon and started eating.

Matilda opened the shop door and the bell made that twinkle sound.

"Be with you in a minute," shouted Mr Dudley, in a muffled voice.

Matilda looked around, and she could not see Mr Dudley. Suddenly, she heard a groaning sound coming from under the counter. She walked over to the counter and peered over.

Matilda could not believe her eyes, Mr Dudley was sitting on the floor with a cardboard box on his head, glitter and ribbons and glue all over the place. Matilda had to put her hand over her mouth so she wouldn't burst out laughing.

"Mr Dudley, would you like some help?"

"Matilda, is that you?"

"Yes, it is."

"Thank goodness."

"Would you mind getting this box off my head and untying my hands? I have gotten into a right muddle with this glitter."

Matilda removed the box from Mr Dudley's head. Her lips started to tremble and she could no longer hold her laughter in. All the glitter had stuck to Mr Dudley's lips and there was pink ribbon in and around his hair. As Mr Dudley coughed, the gold glitter went everywhere.

"Not what you were expecting to find on your first day, hey Matilda," smiled Mr Dudley.

"No," Matilda laughed.

"Now if you would be so kind as to untie this ribbon that somehow I have managed to wrap around my whole body."

"What happened, Mr Dudley?"

"Well, Matilda, I was looking for some Sellotape, and I could not remember where on earth I put it, so I was looking into this box that was on top of this shelf, then the box toppled over and landed on my head, then I tripped over the ribbons and landed on the floor and that's when I started to get tangled up."

"Oh dear, it's a good job you didn't hurt yourself,'" said Matilda.

"Yes, hmm," said Mr Dudley, wrinkling his nose and then sneezing glitter everywhere.

"Bless you," said Matilda.

"Thank you. Well it's a good job you are here to save me then, isn't it Matilda?"

"Yes indeed, Mr Dudley."

"Right, there we are." Mr Dudley jumped up, dusted himself off and looked at Matilda. "Right let's get some work done."

"Mr Dudley."

"Yes."

"You might want to wash your face first," said Matilda, trying not to laugh.

"Really, why Matilda?"

Matilda looked round the shop and saw an old round hand mirror. She picked it up and handed it to Mr Dudley.

"Look," said Matilda.

Mr Dudley pulled the mirror to his face.

"Oh." And he lifted one eyebrow. Gold glitter was still stuck to his lips. "What's wrong with that? Is gold not my colour, dear?" Matilda and Mr Dudley started laughing. Then he started dancing like a ballerina around the shop.

Then suddenly a large banging noise came from upstairs.

"GEORGE DUDLEY, what on earth is all that noise downstairs?"

"Nothing dear, just the usual stuff," winked Mr Dudley.

"Well, whatever, the usual stuff is loud, so keep it down. I am trying to get some rest."

"Yes, dear, no problem."

Matilda was wiping her laughter tears away. She hadn't laughed like that in ages.

"Right that's that, give me ten minutes, Matilda. I just need to wash this glitter off my face."

Matilda started to put the ribbons back in the box. *Oh, Mr Dudley, you do make me laugh,* thought Matilda, smiling to herself.

"Right-oh I am back, Matilda."

Matilda looked up at Mr Dudley. The glitter had gone from his lips but still there was a little sparkle here and there on his face of gold glitter when the light caught him.

"This stuff gets everywhere," said Mr Dudley. "I looked like a Christmas card." He smiled. "Leave that, Matilda. I will clean that up in a minute. Let's get you started in the cellar."

Matilda followed Mr Dudley to the back of the shop where there was a big brown wooden door with a rusty bolt lock on it. Mr Dudley pulled the bolt back and opened the door.

"I must apologise, Matilda, about the mess. I haven't been down here in quite a while."

"That's OK, Mr Dudley."

Mr Dudley reached up and pulled a cord and the light flickered on, Matilda peered down. There were big stone steps leading down and it smelt very musty like no one had been down there in years.

"Follow me," said Mr Dudley in a cheerful voice as they walked further down. Matilda's eyes lit up, there was so much stuff down there. "Right here we are at the bottom, watch your step Matilda, there is stuff everywhere." Matilda looked around, She saw a pile of old dusty books in the corner, a massive chest full of old costume clothes, soldiers' uniforms that looked very old and old fashioned toys, old shoes, jars, plant pots, swords, old magazines, old garden furniture, and much more.

Wow! This cellar is so cool and I can't wait to tidy it up and see what else there is, she thought.

"Right this is my cellar, Matilda." As Mr Dudley pulled his hand down a cobweb had stuck to it, so he wiped it off on his trousers. "Right, as I was saying it's a big job. Are you up for the challenge, Matilda?"

"Of course, I am," said Matilda, smiling.

"Great. Do you see the green boxes over in the corner?"

"Yes."

"Well, these are recycling boxes. You do know what recycling boxes are, Matilda?"

"Yes, I do, Mr Dudley. My grandma recycles."

"Great stuff, right then I would like you to fill up the recycling boxes with all these old magazines or any old bits of paper you find. Now if you need any more green boxes, just shout up the stairs and I will bring you some down, OK, Matilda."

"OK, Mr Dudley."

"Good girl, right-oh, I am off upstairs now to tidy up that glitter and ribbon mess, and remember if you need anything just give me a shout, and have fun!"

Mr Dudley walked back upstairs, whistling a cheerful tune to himself.

Matilda was still looking around the cellar, *Wow this place was exciting.* Every nook and space was filled with something, old wallpapers and old dolls that looked a little scary. The dolls were dressed in old fashioned clothes and their eyes were painted on. Matilda felt that when she moved around the cellar, the dolls' eyes followed her.

"Stop being such a scaredey cat," said Matilda to herself.

Right, let's get started. She looked around and saw the pile of magazines, well more like a mountain of magazines, stacked in the corner leaning against the wall.

Let's start there.

Matilda walked over and picked up a small pile of magazines. She blew the dust off them, which made her sneeze. She looked back down at the magazine, it read: Beano Magazine 1983. She looked at the one underneath and wiped the dust off this one, it read *My Little Pony 1981. Now this magazine looks really cool. Wow these magazines were really old, Mr Dudley must have put them down here when he couldn't sell them in his shop and forgot about them.*

Two hours later, all three containers were filled with recycling. *Wow,* thought Matilda, as she brushed the dust off her jumper. *That was hard work, even my arms are aching.* Matilda looked around, tapping her chin, *still so much to do though.*

"Woo-hoo," said Mr Dudley, clumsily walking down the stairs. "How are you getting on, Matilda?" Mr Dudley shuffled over to Matilda. "Goodness me, you have been busy, what a great job!" said Mr Dudley, looking around proudly at the green containers filled with magazines. "The recycle man, Billy, will be so pleased when he sees all these boxes filled up," smiled Mr Dudley.

Matilda could still see glitter in Mr Dudley's hair. The cellar light caught bits of the glitter, making his hair twinkle.

"Right-oh, Matilda, let's get these boxes up to the shop." Matilda took one box and Mr Dudley took the other box. As they got to the top, Mr Dudley pulled the cord to turn off the light and they walked around to the shop floor.

"Just put the box round the corner please, Matilda." Matilda dropped the box on the floor.

"Wow! My arms are going to be so muscly after all this lifting, Mr Dudley."

"Yes, I imagine they will be Matilda. I bet after you tidy and sort out the whole cellar, you will be the strongest girl in the whole world. No one will mess with the super girl called Muscle-

Matilda, put your arms up!" Matilda started laughing as Mr Dudley was jogging around on the spot boxing in the air.

"One, two, one, two, jab and Mr Dudley wins against his opponent Moody Melvin!" shouted Mr Dudley excitedly.

"GEORGE DUDLEY, what on earth is going on down there?"

"Nothing dear."

"Well, nothing is noisy. Keep it down."

"Yes, dear."

Mr Dudley pulled a funny face and Matilda giggled.

"Right, Muscle-Matilda, you get the last box and bring it up here, because your legs are younger than mine," laughed Mr Dudley. "And I will make you a sandwich and drink. It's thirsty work, all this lifting and sorting."

Matilda pulled the cord to turn on the light, then walked down the stairs. She walked over to the green boxes, but something caught Matilda's eye in the far corner. Matilda squinted her eyes. *There is something over there glittering in the back corner, there is something under that dusty old sheet.* It was shiny red, Matilda walked a bit closer and was about to pull off the dusty old sheet...

"MATLIDA!" shouted Mr Dudley. "Your sandwich and drink are ready."

Matilda stopped, *well I am rather hungry. Oh well, whatever it is will have to wait.* Matilda lifted up the green box with a sigh, *thank goodness this is the last book, my arms are so tired.*

"Here you go, super girl," laughed Mr Dudley, handing Matilda a glass of pineapple juice and a cheese and pickle sandwich.

"Thank you, Mr Dudley."

"You're welcome, Matilda."

Matilda picked up her pineapple juice and took two massive gulps. She put her glass down and took a bite of her cheese and pickle sandwich. *Hmm, that is so good,* thought Matilda, *just what I needed.*

"Mr Dudley, how come you have so much stuff in your cellar?"

Mr Dudley peered over his newspaper.

"What an interesting question. Some stuff is from the shop, and Mrs Dudley, but the old hats and puppets etc. are from my travels as a young man."

Mr Dudley suddenly threw the paper on the shop counter and stood up.

"But no ordinary travels, Matilda. Magical travels, into another world where anything is possible, and the normal is not normal. You would be in shock with amazement. I have danced like an Egyptian in Egypt, and had tea with pharaohs, gone ice-skating with bears in Russia, talked to puppets in Prague, helped make toys with elves in the North Pole... so many adventures. So many happy times," grinned Mr Dudley, as he stared into the distance, as if remembering something special.

Matilda just looked at Mr Dudley with her mouth open and a half-chewed sandwich still in her mouth.

Suddenly, the shop bell twinkled and Mrs Bumble walked in.

"Afternoon, everybody. Matilda, do close your mouth when you are eating, I can see your half chewed sandwich." Matilda blinked then closed her mouth.

"Afternoon, Mrs Bumble. What can I do for you today?"

Matilda finished chewing her bit of sandwich and then picked her pineapple juice up and took another gulp. *Wow* thought Matilda, *I have never seen Mr Dudley so excited and full of life before, but what on earth was he going on about? Ice-skating with bears in Russia and talking to puppets in Prague? Mr Dudley and his imagination. What a funny man.*

Mrs Bumble handed Mr Dudley some money for her shopping and then said goodbye to Mr Dudley. She then walked over to Matilda.

"Give your grandma my kindest regards, Matilda, please, and tell her I will pop over during the week. I have some cake recipes that she may like."

"OK, Mrs Bumble."

"OK, thanks, Matilda. Bye."

"Right," said Mr Dudley, with a big grin. "I think that's enough excitement for today." He reached into his pocket and pulled out a five-pound note. "Here you go, Matilda, for a hard day's work."

"Thank you, Mr Dudley."

"No Matilda, thank you. Now you'd better get on your way. Your grandma will be wondering where you are. I will see you tomorrow, bright and early," he winked.

Matilda reached to open the front door, when suddenly her grandma opened the door singing, "If you like it then you better put a ring on it." Matilda just stared while her grandma waved her hand in front of her face.

"I hope you don't mind Matilda, I borrowed one of your CDs. I quite like this Beyoncé lady." Matilda's lips started twitching, then a roar of laughter came out. Her grandma stopped dancing and said she quite liked this hop-hip stuff. Matilda was wiping away her laughter tears.

"Grandma, it's hip-hop not hop-hip."

"Oh right, word up. Come on Matilda, your dinner is nearly ready, Matilda walked through the door, and took off her rain coat, still smiling.

"Grandma, I saw Mrs Bumble. She said to say hi and that she will be round during the week with some new cake recipes."

"Oh lovely."

I dread to think what tomorrow brings, especially if she listens to one of my Lady Gaga CDs, giggled Matilda.

Matilda woke up to the ringing of alarm bells. She rolled over, slammed her hand on the alarm and said under her breath, "Five more minutes," and pulled the covers over her head. *Brr, it's even colder than yesterday.* Suddenly, Matilda's bedroom door opened and Grandma started singing "Run the world" at the top of her voice, Matilda peered over the covers.

"Still listening to Beyoncé again, Grandma?"

"Well, yes dear. Just making sure you are up dear, and breakfast is ready so get a shuffle on."

Matilda arrived at the shop ten minutes early. She was very excited to get back down to the cellar and see what else was down there. She walked through the shop door and the bell tinkled. Matilda could not see anyone in the shop.

"Hello, Mr Dudley, are you there?"

Mr Dudley popped his head up from behind the shop counter wearing the furriest hat Matilda had ever seen.

"Hello Matilda. Do you like my hat? It's a raccoon hat." He turned around and showed Matilda the tail.

"Gross."

"What, don't you like it, Matilda? It's my exploring hat."

"It's OK, I guess, but not my style," said Matilda. "But why are you wearing your exploring hat in the shop?"

"Well, isn't it obvious? I am exploring the shop, looking for some paperclips. I can't find them anywhere, so I thought this hat might help me."

"Well, has it helped you?" said Matilda.

"Hmm, erm," said Mr Dudley while tapping his chin with his finger. "Well, no."

Matilda started laughing.

Mr Dudley took his hat off and threw it in the corner while laughing. The hat hit a drawer and the drawer fell on the floor and a tub of paperclips rolled over to Mr Dudley's feet.

"AH HA, see, the hat worked."

Matilda looked astonished.

"That is amazing."

"You just have to believe, Matilda, that is all, and once you believe, anything is possible."

Matilda nodded.

"Right, let's get to it. I have some paperwork to do up here. You know where you're going, don't you, Matilda?"

"Yes, Mr Dudley."

"Great. Down the cellar is a big blue chest. It's full of old clothes. Next to the chest are four full boxes of old clothes as well. Here are four bags. Can you separate out the good clothes and put them in this pink bag, and the clothes that are unusable, put them in this blue bag. I know it's a lot to do."

"It's fine, Mr Dudley, no problem."

"Good girl," smiled Mr Dudley.

Matilda grabbed the bags and made her way to the cellar door. She opened the door and pulled the light cord and made her way down the stone steps. That musty smell hit Matilda's nostrils again. *Phew.* Matilda put the bags on an old wooden table, put her hands on her hips and said to herself, "Where is that blue chest?" A sparkle caught Matilda's eye again. *Aha! That's what I was going to look at yesterday, that glittery red thing under that dusty old sheet.*

Matilda walked to the corner and gently pulled off the dusty sheet. *Wow,* mouthed Matilda. Underneath was the most beautiful bike she had ever seen in her life.

It was a beautiful shiny bright red bike that glittered in the cellar light, like it had its own magical glow. It had pearl handles, bright white tyres, a gold bike chain that was so shiny you could see yourself in it and red peddles; Matilda stared at the bike. *This bike looks brand new, like it has never been touched. What is a beautiful bike like this doing down here and underneath an old dusty sheet?* Matilda suddenly saw an envelope sticking out the back of the leather seat. She reached for the envelope and picked it up and turned the envelope around. In red glittering writing was her name, Matilda Marsh. *What on earth? That's my name.* Matilda stared at the envelope. *Well, it's not my birthday but I don't know anyone else called Matilda Marsh.* Matilda slowly opened the envelope and pulled a glowing white piece of paper out. Even the paper was beautiful, with gold spiral swirls. She cleared her throat and read what the gold glittering writing said...

To find an adventure you only have to make one, to find something that's lost you just have to believe you will find it.

Good luck, T.M.

T.M., who is T.M and what does this letter mean? To make an adventure and find something that is lost? What on earth is going on? Matilda put the letter in her pocket and walked round the bike to see if she could find anything else. *Hmm,* she thought. *What if I sit on it? Well, that's*

got to be the most comfortable bike seat I have ever sat on. Let's see if the bike works. Matilda kicked up the bike pole that the bike was leaning on and started to peddle across the cellar.

Suddenly, sparks started to fly out of the tyres and the bike lifted off the ground and everything started to swirl round really fast. *What's happening?* Matilda firmly held onto the pearl handles, her knuckles went white from grabbing them too tight. Suddenly, there were flashes of colour and popping, cracking and whizzing noises from every direction. Matilda shut her eyes and started screaming, it was like being on the scariest roller coaster with no safety features and not knowing when it's going to stop.

Suddenly, the bike dropped onto a hard floor and Matilda opened her eyes.

"Aaah!" screamed Matilda .She was heading straight to a big pond. She quickly squeezed her brakes as hard as she could, and the bike's back wheel went skidding everywhere. Matilda just managed to stop the bike just at the edge of the big pond. She quickly kicked out the bike pole and got off the bike. Her hands was still shaking and she was trying to get her breath back. *What just happened? I still feel a little bit dizzy. Am I dreaming?* She pinched herself. *Ouch, no I am wide awake.* Matilda looked round for moment, "Where am I?" She said to herself. In front of Matilda, there was a massive pond with lily pads and underneath the water, Matilda could see colourful fish swimming and the sunlight catching their scales making them glitter. Beyond the pond was a massive forest with multi-coloured trees; pink, blue, orange and purple. Matilda rubbed her eyes and looked again. *Nope, I was right the first time. That tree is definitely purple.* In the far distance, there were massive mountains that looked like ice-cream cones. To her left was a small stone path which looked like it led to a small town.

Right, first thing is first. I need to find out where I am...

"Hello," said a small voice. Matilda quickly looked round and could not see anybody.

"No silly, look down, I am down here in the pond." Matilda looked down and jumped back. "Hello, I am Tony Toad, the Guardian of Water. Lovely to make your acquaintance," he said, while sitting on his lily pad near the edge of the pond.

You can talk? A talking toad? A toad that talks? I think I'd better sit down by that tree, I must have banged my head or something. I am looking at a multi-coloured forest, with a toad

talking to me. It's finally happened, I have gone mad. She put her head in her hands.

Tony hopped off the lily pad and made his way to Matilda.

"Excuse me, are you OK?"

Matilda looked up.

"Not really sure, Tony."

"Well, my friend, is there anything I can help you with?"

"Do you know, where I am?"

"Well, of course I do. You are in Old Magic Prague."

"Hmm," said Matilda. "Right, where exactly is Old Magic Prague?" asked Matilda.

"Well, it's in Prague, silly."

"Oh, of course," said Matilda.

"You are a human?"

"Yes, yes," said Matilda.

"Well, we haven't had a human visit Old Magic Prague in years. The last human was a little boy called, erm, for the life of me I can't remember his name. Well, I am sure it will come back to me. So how did you get here?

"Well, I am not really sure to be honest. I found this bike with a letter addressed to me, sat on the bike, started to peddle and ended up here."

"Wow! A magic bike," said Tony. "I haven't heard of a magic bike since that human boy. If only I could remember his name. Where is your bike now?" asked Tony the Toad.

Matilda went over to where it was. She jumped up.

"It's gone!"

"Where has it gone?"

"Oh no, how on earth am I ever going to get back?"

"Don't worry," said Tony the Toad. "I will contact Mr Hobble. He is the Wise Guardian of Old Magic Prague. He lives in the town down there, just follow the stone path and you will see an old book shop called 'Knowledge to All Who Seek It.' I will let Mr Hobble know that he is expecting a visitor."

Matilda looked at Tony the Toad.

"How will you do that?"

"A bubble burp."

"A what?"

"A bubble burp. It's really simple. I make a bubble in my throat and I record a message in it and burp it out. It then floats to who I send it to. Look!" said Tony the Toad. He jumped back to his lily pad and sat up very straight. "Right, here goes." Suddenly Tony the Toad's outside throat skin stretched as big as a tennis ball and then he let out an almighty burp! And this bubble popped out. Tony spoke to the bubble and sent it to Mr Hobble's house.

"See it's that easy."

"That is the most amazing thing I have ever seen said." Matilda was astonished.

"Well, why, thank you, Matilda but that is how everybody contacts each other here."

"What about phones?"

"Phones?" said Tony. "What is that?"

"That's what we use to contact people."

"Phones, hey. Sounds fancy." Suddenly, a bubble burp appeared in front of Matilda. "Ah Matilda, you have your first bubble burp."

"What do I do with it?"

"You pop it with your finger, my dear, and listen."

Matilda reached up and popped it with her finger. Suddenly she heard a very old excited voice say, "Welcome, Matilda, to Old Magic Prague. We haven't had a human for years! Your timing is impeccable! Now Tony Toad has told me all about you and you must come quickly as we have much to talk about. I have put on some rhubarb tea and I have some custard cake because I am sure you will be hungry after your travels. Bye now."

"That bubble burp is so cool," said Matilda.

"Well, Matilda, I wish you well on your journey and it was a pleasure to meet you."

"And it was a pleasure to meet you Tony the Toad, Guardian of the Water."

Tony took a bow and Matilda giggled.

"Bye, Tony Toad."

"Bye, Matilda. Come and visit again soon."

Matilda waved and followed the stone path into town. *Well I wanted an adventure,* smiled Matilda to herself. On Matilda's way down the stone path, she saw an apple cart toppled over and a half-goblin and half-elf man rushing around picking up the apples, Matilda walked over.

"Can I help you?"

The half-elf and half-goblin stood up. He had bright wild orange hair, big wide blue eyes, and he looked young in the face. He wore a pair of apple-patterned dungarees with a multi-coloured T-shirt.

"Well my, my, a human. Haven't seen one of them in a while." He smiled. "Welcome, my friend, to Old Magic Prague. I am Oak Elfling, Guardian of the Forest and Fruit. Lovely to make your acquaintance. And you are?"

"My name is Matilda."

"Matilda, what a lovely name," said Oak.

"Thank you," smiled Matilda. "What happened to your apple cart?"

"Well, my friend," said Oak. "I was pushing the cart into town and the wheel fell off and some of the applejacks escaped onto the floor."

"Oh dear," said Matilda. "I can help you fix it. If I lift up the cart you can push the wheel back on."

"Excellent thinking," said Oak.

Matilda lifted the cart with all her strength and Oak pushed the wheel on and locked it in place.

"As good as new," said Oak. "Well, thank you, Matilda. You are very kind. Here, have an applejack." Matilda looked at the applejack, it was red on one side and green on the other. Matilda took a bite of the green side.

"Nooo wait, not like that," said Oak. Suddenly, Matilda scrunched her face up. It was sourer than a lemon. Oak burst out laughing. "Sour, isn't it? Oh boy, I remember that taste, yuk." Matilda nodded, trying to swallow the sour piece of applejack. "Quickly bite the red side," said Oak. Matilda bit into the red side of the applejack and immediately the sour went away and she had the most sweet, juicy-tasting apple she had ever tasted in her life.

"Well, that was interesting," said Matilda. Oak laughed.

"Sorry about that. I should have told you straight away but you were so fast in putting the applejack in your mouth, I didn't have time, you see. Matilda, this is a special fruit used for many things. It comes from the pink trees in the forest. The green side of the apple jack is so sour it could turn your face inside-out," laughed Oak.

"It almost did," said Matilda. "Good job I only took a small bite."

"Yes indeed, and the red side is the sweetest juicy taste you will ever taste. Some even find it too sweet so they cut it up into slices and eat one sweet slice and one sour slice together at the same time. It balances the flavours out and tastes amazing. See, I'll show you." Oak pulled out his little knife and cut two slices for Matilda, one green and one red. "See, now, put both in your mouth at the same time."

Matilda popped the two slices of applejack in her mouth.

"Wow! That tastes incredible. Absolutely delicious. Oak, thank you."

"Glad you liked it," smiled Oak proudly.

"So do all the different coloured trees have different fruits?"

"Why, yes, they do. So the pink trees as you now know, grow applejacks. As soon as you pick a fruit it grows back three days later. The purple tree grows cocoa grapes, half chocolate and half grape. The blue tree grows bananas, half banana half nut, and the orange tree grows orange juice."

"Orange juice? How is that even possible?"

"Well, you pick the orange from the tree, you poke a wooden straw in it and drink the orange juice straight from the fruit. Once you have drunk the orange juice, you eat it. Yes, it tastes like orange cake."

"Orange cake, that sounds brilliant," said Matilda.

"Yes, a lot of Elflings like this one and the cocoa grapes as they have very sweet teeth."

"These trees are amazing to grow these types of fruits."

"Well," said Oak in a hushed voice, "legend has it that the wind herself carried these seeds from the giant ice-cream mountains, where the multi-coloured giants live and then they landed on an open plain. A forest started to grow different-coloured trees within three days of the seeds landing there.

"How interesting," said Matilda. "Are the giants friendly?"

"No they are not. They have stolen all the magic puppet strings from town. Old Magic Prague is famous for its puppet shows. All you could hear was laughter from miles away from the Elflings and the Elflings' children, and now the puppets sit there with no life in them because their magic strings were taken from them by Frightful Freddie."

"Wow, he sounds like a scary giant."

"He is my dear. Let me tell you, oh, you have a bubble burp." Matilda popped the bubble with her finger...

"Matilda, do hurry child, your rhubarb tea is getting cold."

"You'd best be on your way," said Oak. "Lovely to meet you and thanks for your help."

"You're welcome," said Matilda. She quickly picked up her pace along the stone path.

She made it into town. It was very quiet and no one was around. It was like an old fashioned town, like something out of a fairy tale, different-coloured window shutters on cute little cottages, stone paths leading in every direction, little stone bridges leading over the small streams, small carts of hay in the corner, empty market stalls. *Right, where is that bookshop,* thought Matilda, looking around. *Aha, there it is.* The bookshop with the sign saying 'Knowledge to All That Seek It.' *Wow what a lovely-looking building.* It has big blue wooden shutters and a big wooden blue door with a sign on it saying 'All are welcome'.

Matilda walked over to the door and knocked on it. The door opened and there stood an old Elfling with a long grey beard, to his knees, wearing a long blue coat with a baggy old fashioned shirt.

"Welcome, my dear Matilda. I am Mr Hobbles, the Guardian of the Wise. Lovely to finally make your acquaintance. Come in my dear and have some rhubarb tea."

He shuffled Matilda through the dusty old bookshop and into the back room and behind a long velvet dusty curtain to a little old blue chair.

"Sit, Matilda, please."

Matilda sat on the blue chair and Mr Hobbles pulled up a red old chair which was very tatty in parts, but she thought it suited the old bookshop look.

"Well, my dear, I have been hearing good things along the way about you through bubble burp. Tony the Toad and Oak speak very highly of you. There is much talk among all the Guardians about you.

"Wow, really?" said Matilda, surprised.

"Yes, my dear. Elflings love a good gossip and it's not every day a human comes to Old Magic Prague."

"Mr Hobbles, can I ask a question?"

"Of course Matilda, ask away, my dear."

"How come you have so many Guardians?"

Mr Hobbles laughed and his little round belly shook as he laughed.

"Well Matilda, we all have a job in this life to look after one another and care for things. Well, the job really chooses us we do not choose the job."

"How does the job choose you then?" asked Matilda, puzzled.

"Well, that's easy. It's through your heart and love of things. Take Oak. Ever since he was an Elfling child he played and cared for the forest and picked the fruit for the Elflings of Old Magic Prague without even being asked to. As he got older, he built a treehouse in the forest because he loved being in the forest so much. See, he listened to his heart and became Guardian of the Forest and Fruit, and Tony the Toad wasn't always a toad, he was an Elfling, but he loved the water so much he kept wishing and believing he would one day live on the lily pads in the big pond. And one day he woke up as a toad, and he has never been as happy as he is in the water. As for me, well, my love for books and knowledge has made me very wise. As long as you are true to yourself and true to what you love in your heart, you can become a Guardian. You Matilda, what do you love to do? What's in your heart?" asked Mr Hobbles.

"I love learning about all the different herbs and the natural medicine that can heal people, like what my parents taught me," sighed Matilda.

"Ahh yes, your parents, very special people. Don't worry, Matilda, your parents will find their way back to you one day."

"How did you know about my parents, Mr Hobbles?"

"Ahh, I am the Guardian of the Wise," he winked. "There's not much I don't know," he smiled. "Well Matilda that makes you the Guardian of Healers."

Matilda smiled.

"I like the sound of that."

"So do I," said Mr Hobbles., "Right, goodness me, I almost forgot the rhubarb tea and custard cake." Mr Hobbles quickly sat up from his chair, walked into the next room and wheeled out a teapot and cups with a bright small yellow bits of custard cake. Mr Hobbles poured the rhubarb tea into the cup. It was bright red. The smell filled Matilda's nostrils.

"That smells delightful, Mr Hobbles."

"Well, thank you, Matilda. I am famous around Old Magic Prague for my rhubarb tea," he smiled. "OK Matilda, what you have to do now is drop your small bit of custard cake in the rhubarb tea and stir round three times."

"Really?" said Matilda.

"Yes, Matilda. This is how we drink tea and cake."

Matilda picked up the custard cake and plopped it in the rhubarb tea and stirred three times. The colour changed instantly to a reddy-creamy colour. Matilda put the cup to her lips and drank. There was an explosion of flavour in her mouth. The tangy rhubarb and creamy taste of the custard and the sweet taste of the cake.

"This has to be the best rhubarb and custard I have ever had."

"Well, I did tell you I was famous for it."

"And I can see why," said Matilda.

"Well, if you think that's nice you should try my applejack tea. Took me two years to get that recipe right. First the tea was too sour then the tea was too sweet. But once I perfected it, it was scrummy and I drank about five cups a day. I had to stop myself drinking so much," Mr Hobbles laughed. "At the moment, I am working on another hot drink with the chocolate and

grape. Hot chocolate grape! The Elflings will love this one. Well, look at me talking your ears off."

"Oh, I don't mind," said Matilda. "I find this all very interesting."

"Bless you," said Mr Hobbles. "But Tony the Toad said you needed help?"

"Well, yes. I came here on a magic bike, and now the magic bike has disappeared but I need to get home."

"Right, let me consult the books. I saw something a few years back about a magic bike." Mr Hobbles walked out to the bookshop. A minute later, he came back with a big dusty leather book called *Magicus.* He sat back down on his chair and stated flicking through the pages muttering to himself. "Aha, yes, here it is." Mr Hobbles showed the page of the magic bike to Matilda. "Is that your bike, Matilda?

Matilda looked at the picture.

"Yes, it is," she said. "Exactly. What does it say about it, Mr Hobbles?"

"Well, it's the most magical bike in all the worlds. It was sent to you by a very powerful magician."

"But I don't know any magicians," said Matilda.

"You probably do, Matilda, without even knowing it. Magicians are the Guardians of All Magic, but like to keep themselves to themselves for many reasons. They visit human worlds all the time and try to help people who need it. They go under cover as teachers, police officers, shop keepers, chefs, and bin men. You have probably met at least six magicians without even realising it. Clever people, magicians."

"Crikey, that's astonishing."

"I know," laughed Mr Hobbles. "He looked back down at the book. It says the bike will appear and disappear when it wants to. It will appear when it feels you are ready to come home or go on another adventure, and when the bike feels like your heart is complete, it will disappear for ever. Magic bikes have a mind of their own, you see, Matilda. A magician sent you the magic bike but it's up to the magic bike, what it wants to do with you and where to take you."

"Well, how long is that going to take? My grandma will start worrying about me and Mr Dudley will be upset that I haven't cleaned the cellar."

"Don't get upset, Matilda. Everything will be OK, trust me, I am the Guardian of the wise."

"OK, Mr Hobbles. Well, I just have to wait for the magic bike to appear again, I guess," Matilda said, whilst picking up her cup and having another gulp of rhubarb tea with custard. "Hmm," said Matilda. Mr Hobbles shut the book and put to one side.

"Matilda, I need your help. You are the first human we have had here in a very long time. Do you know about Frightful Freddie?"

"Oh, yes I do. Oak told me all about how he stole the magic strings and how all the puppets are lifeless."

"Yes, that's correct. You see Elflings are very happy creatures and very sensitive. Did you notice on your way down that the town was very quiet and there were no other Elflings about?"

"Yes, I did think it was a bit quiet to be honest."

"Well, since Frightful Freddie took the magic strings, the Elflings have been very sad. Indeed, so sad that they don't come out of their cottages or even go to work in the markets anymore. And it's only getting worse and I am getting very worried about Old Magic Prague. I know it's a lot to ask of you, Matilda, but I know that if anyone can do it, it will be you. Can you go to Ice-cream Mountain and get our magic strings back from Frightful Freddie?"

Matilda just stared at Mr Hobbles for a while, taking in what he had just said. Matilda stood up.

"You other Elflings have been so kind to me. It will be my honour to help you, Mr Hobbles."

Mr Hobbles jumped up and hugged Matilda tight.

"Thank you so much, Matilda. I knew you would not let us down." Mr Hobbles suddenly let go of Matilda. "Right, I better pack you a bag and you will need a warm coat and hat, as Ice-cream Mountain gets very cold and you need a map to Frightful Freddie's cave. I will get Oak to take you through the multi-coloured forest. Can you bubbleburp him, Matilda?"

"I have never done a bubbleburp, Mr Hobbles."

"Yes, of course you haven't. Hmm, it's very easy. Wait I have something that can help you." He went to the back of the room and opened a cupboard. Inside was little tiny bottles of different coloured liquids. "Here it is, fizzy bubbly boo. This is the bubbliest liquid in all of Old Magic Prague, useful for many things, especially first time bubble-burpers." Mr Hobbles handed Matilda the liquid. "Right, Matilda, take one drop on your tongue, no more than one, otherwise it will turn in to a bottom burp, not bubble burp."

"OK," said Matilda. "Here goes." She squeezed the end of the dropstick to suck up the liquid. She pulled the dropstick out and squeezed gently. One drop fell on her tongue. Suddenly, it started to fizz and foam.

"Right Matilda, now swallow." Matilda swallowed and suddenly it felt like she had just drunk four cans of fizzy pop.

"I need to burp, Mr Hobbles."

"OK Matilda, burp and think of a bubble." Matilda closed her eyes, thought about a bubble, and burped the loudest burp she had ever burped. "That was excellent, Matilda." Matilda opened her eyes and in front of her face was a large bubble. "Now talk to the bubble and send it to Oak."

"Hi Oak," Matilda said. "Can you come to Mr Hobbles' bookshop? We need your help. Thanks, Matilda. Bubbleburp can you go to Oak, please?"

The bubbleburp floated through the bookshop and went out through the window.

"Well done, Matilda."

Matilda smiled.

"That wasn't so bad."

Mr Hobbles went out the room and came back in.

"Right here is a map." It was a rolled piece of old paper. "Here is a coat." Mr Hobbles handed Matilda a patchwork quilted jacket with a hat to match.

"This is beautiful, Mr Hobbles."

"Thank you, Matilda. I made it myself. Mrs Thread the Guardian of Sewing showed me how to do it." Suddenly, there was knocking at the door. Mr Hobbles went through the curtain to the front door. He came in two minutes later with Oak.

"Hi Matilda, I got your bubble burp. What's the matter? Hmm, do I smell rhubarb tea with custard cake?"

"I will get you a cup, Oak." Mr Hobble brought a cup and saucer over to Oak. Oak poured the rhubarb tea in the cup, added the custard cake and stirred three times.

"Have you got any sugar syrup?" asked Oak.

"Yes, I will grab you a bottle."

"What is sugar syrup, Oak?"

"Sugar syrup is sweeter than sugar. I have two drops in my rhubarb tea. Us Elflings have a sweet tooth you know." Mr Hobbles walked back in with a little bottle and put it next to the fizzy bubbly boo.

"Oak, I need your help. Matilda has agreed to help us get our magic strings back. I can't wait any longer, the Elflings are getting more unhappy as each day passes."

"And Matilda, are you OK with this?" asked Oak.

"Yes I am; you all have been so kind, I just want to help you all."

Oak smiled.

"You are the bravest girl I have ever met."

Mr Hobbles opened the map and put two stones on each end to keep the map open.

"I need you, Oak, to take Matilda through the multi-coloured forest to Ice-cream Mountain."

"No problem, Mr Hobbles. That's the least I can do."

Oak turned around and picked up the bottle and put two drops of liquid in his rhubarb tea and quickly drank it.

"Hmm." Mr Hobbles rolled up the map and put it into a large satchel. He then folded the patchwork jacket and rolled up the hat and placed them in the bag. Suddenly, Oak grabbed his stomach, where gurgling and moaning sounds started to come from.

"What was in that tea, Mr Hobbles?"

"Nothing! Just rhubarb and custard cake."

"Oh no," said Matilda. "What liquid did you put in your tea?"

"Only this sugar syrup bottle."

"No, that's fizzy bubbly boo," said Matilda. "You picked up the wrong bottle, Oak."

"Oh dear," said Oak in a nervous voice. "How many drops did you put in, Oak?"

"Only two, Mr Hobbles."

"Oh no, well, nothing we can do now except to take cover. Matilda, get under the table with me."

Oak's stomach started to get bigger and bigger and bigger.

"It looks like he is going to pop. Matilda, this is called a bottom burp. Get ready, he is about to go!" Suddenly, Oak let out a massive squeak and then a massive sound came out of his bottom. Oak was bouncing all over the place, up and down, turning in all directions. Matilda's eyes could not keep up with him, he was going so fast all over the place. Matilda heard one more squeak then, bang! Oak fell to the floor. Mr Hobbles and Matilda ran over to him.

"Are you OK, Oak?"

"I feel a little funny, to be honest." Mr Hobbles put Oak in the old chair.

"He will be OK in a minute. You see, Matilda, the bottom burp works like a balloon. You know when you blow a balloon up and then let go of it? It's the same thing. The bubbles swell your stomach and the only way to get the air out is through your bottom. It can be a messy business, Matilda, let me tell you."

Matilda giggled.

"Will Oak be OK, Mr Hobbles?"

"He will be fine."

"How are you feeling, Oak?"

Oak stood up shook his head.

"A lot better than I did five minutes ago," he laughed.

"OK, Mr Hobbles, are we packed and ready to go?"

"We are, Oak."

"OK, Matilda, here is the satchel. The map is in there. I have put some tutti-frutti bread in there for you in case you get hungry, and a flask of applejack tea."

"Thank you, Mr Hobbles."

"Now, take care and keep in contact through the bubble burp. Stay safe Matilda, and thank you again." Mr Hobbles had tears in his eyes.

"Don't get upset, Mr Hobbles, I will be fine."

"I know you will, Matilda, I know you will."

Oak and Mr Hobbles hugged.

"Be safe, my friend, and look after our Guardian healer."

"I will, don't worry."

Mr Hobbles opened the blue door and Oak and Matilda walked out onto the stone path. They waved back at Mr Hobbles and made their way towards the multi-coloured forest.

Matilda and Oak reached the pond where Matilda first arrived on her bike. Tony the Toad was lying on a lily pad snoozing as the sun was setting behind Ice-cream Mountains.

"Hello, Tony."

Tony opened one eye and yawned.

"Why, hello Matilda, hello Oak. On your way to Ice-cream Mountain, I hear."

"How did you, oh I know, bubble burp."

"Yes, Mr Hobbles has bubble burped the town. You know Elflings, they love to gossip, especially about a brave human who will make Old Prague happy again."

"Good luck on your journey, Matilda and Oak."

Matilda and Oak waved goodbye to Tony Toad and headed to the multi-coloured forest.

"It will be getting dark soon, Matilda, so we will sleep in my treehouse tonight and I will walk you to the bottom of the Ice-cream Mountains in the morning."

"That's good with me, Oak. I am feeling quite tired actually."

"I bet you are."

Oak led Matilda through the multi-coloured forest and it was the most beautiful place she had ever seen and been to. There were the colours and shape of the leaves on trees with bits of faded sunlight shining through, beautiful colourful butterflies with eight wings flying around Matilda's head playing with her, woodlice with their colourful shells playing which looked like bowling balls. One woodlouse was rolled up and the others stood on their feet looking like bowling pins. Then a pink woodlouse threw the rolled up one down towards the pins and knocked over three.

"How's your game, Marg," asked Oak. "Could be better. I need more practice if we are going to beat the Bootleg Beatles."

"I am sure you will win," laughed Oak. The birds are singing... wait a minute, that bird is actually singing with words.

"Oak, that bird is singing."

"Well, of course, Matilda, birds love to sing."

"But with words."

"Yes, don't birds sing where you're from?"

"Yes, but not singing the words, more of a tune really."

"Maybe they do sing with words, but you just don't understand what they sing," said Oak.

"That could be true, I suppose," smiled Matilda. "I never thought of that."

"All forests are magical in every land, Matilda, every creature and plant has its own special super power. You just have to look and listen carefully and understand them. Take the woodlouse. Did you know that woodlice are beneficial to you humans because they eliminate decaying plant material and increase the fertility of the soil and are the only crustaceans that are adapted to the life on the ground? Other crustaceans spend their life in or near water?"

"Wow, that's amazing. I see them all the time in Long Ashton in the forest but just walk past them," said Matilda.

"Well, you see you just have to look and listen. Amazing things are everywhere."

"Oak, are those cornflowers?"

"Yes, they are, Matilda. We call them Bluebottles. We use them to treat wounds in Old Magic Prague."

"I have read about them in my mum and dad's book but never seen one. Can I pick one please, Oak?"

"Help yourself, Matilda. Take as many as you want. When you pick anything in the forest it grows back three days later."

Matilda picked four and put them in her satchel.

"We are here. Welcome to my home." There was a ladder made of different types of wood. "Follow me, Matilda." Matilda looked up.

"That is high." Matilda climbed the ladder and they suddenly reached an egg shaped house. Oak climbed through the curtain into the egg, Matilda followed him.

It was larger than Matilda thought it would be, with two hammocks, a wooden table with four little wooden stools with a magnifying glass on an open book. There were cups that looked like acorn cups, a bookshelf full of books with herbs hanging up everywhere, a stack of candles in the corner and a brush made of twigs in the corner that looked like a Witches' broom.

"Oak I think your home is beautiful."

"Thank you Matilda."

"I built it myself. I studied how birds built their nests and used the same process with twigs and fur from the frizzy plants that grow near the lakes. The frizzy plants shed lots of fur and the Elflings use the fur to make clothes and stuff their bed mattresses with. The forest provides everything you need really."

"I would love to live in a house like this," Matilda smiled.

Suddenly Matilda's stomach started making rumbling noises.

Matilda went into her satchel and pulled out the flask of applejack tea and tutti-frutti bread.

"Are you hungry, Oak?"

"Yes, I am." Oak went down the ladder and came back up with his hands full.

"Right, Matilda, here are two banana nut leaves. These are our plates and two fresh acorn cups for our tea." Oak pulled out his knife and cut the bread and poured the applejack tea into acorn cups.

"Thank you, Oak."

Matilda took a bite of the tutti-frutti bread.

"This is delicious, Oak."

"Yes, Mr Hobbles does bake a good tutti-frutti loaf. It has banana nut in it. The chocolate side of the grape, a splash of orange juice in it and many different nuts and seeds in it. With every bite you taste something different."

Matilda washed down the bread with the applejack tea. When she drank, it was like having a warm hug from the inside. Oak stood up and grabbed two candles, he opened up the window flap and whistled. Suddenly, a tiny fly appeared.

"Would you be so kind?" The fly flew in and went to the candlewick. The fly burped and a flame came out of its mouth. It lit both candles then flew back out the window.

"What was that?" asked Matilda.

"That was a firefly."

"A firefly, of course," said Matilda.

Oak, put the candles in tiny oak cup cases and then put them on the table.

"That's better, I can see you now," he laughed.

"Oak, don't you ever get lonely out here on your own?"

"Why, no, Matilda I am not on my own. The forest and all the animals are my friends and neighbours, I am always busy collecting fruit for the Elflings and researching and collecting different plants."

"Yes, I can see you keep very busy."

"Do you get lonely, Matilda?"

"Sometimes I do. I miss my mum and dad a lot. Mr Hobbles said one day we will find our way back to each other."

"Well, you should listen to Mr Hobbles. He is a very wise man," Oak smiled.

Oak yawned.

"We better get to bed, we have a long walk tomorrow."

Matilda climbed into the hammock and pulled a patchwork blanket over herself. "Goodnight, Oak."

"Goodnight, Matilda." Oak blew out the candles and climbed into his hammock.

Matilda awoke to Oak humming and the birds singing loudly about sunrise and the dew on a leaf.

Oak turned around.

"Good morning, Matilda."

Matilda stretched.

"Good morning," she said half sleepily.

"How did you sleep?"

"Really well. The hammock is so comfy."

"I got us breakfast."

Matilda climbed out of the hammock and sat on the wooden stool. Oak placed a leaf in front of her.

"For your delight this morning we have banana nut, Matilda, with fresh orange juice." Oak poked a wooden straw into an orange and gave it to Matilda. She took a sip.

"Wow, that is the freshest orange juice."

"Good, isn't it?" said Oak. Matilda nodded. Matilda looked at the banana nut and laughed.

"It really is half banana and half nut like a walnut. Tricky things to open."

"Matilda, you peel one side and crack open the other side with this long nut cracker but you have to be careful because sometimes you squash the banana," Oak laughed.

Matilda popped the banana nut in her mouth and started chewing.

"Hmm."

After breakfast, Oak packed a little bag with different fruits wrapped in leaves.

"I do wish I had a hairbrush," said Matilda.

Oak went outside and came back in two minutes later.

"Here." He threw a pinecone at Matilda.

"What's this?"

"Nature's hairbrush. Go on, brush your hair with it."

"OK, I will try it but I don't think it is going to work."

Matilda put the pinecone to her hair and started brushing.

"It works."

"Well, of course, you can keep that one I have loads."

"Thank you, Oak."

Matilda and Oak made their way down the ladder onwards to Ice-cream Mountain.

"We shall rest here by the stream and have food." They sat under a massive Oak tree. Oak pulled out two oak cups, filled them with water by the stream, and pulled out the fruit wrapped in the leaves. He shared the fruit and gave Matilda her leaf. Matilda put the leaf down, took her shoes and socks off and picked up the leaf and went over to the stream and put her feet into it.

"Ahh, that's better." Suddenly, she saw loads of sea horses splashing around near her feet jumping on them then jumping off.

"Matilda." Oak walked over. "Ah, you found the lake horses. They love to play and eat." Oak threw some banana nut in the water and the lake horses raced over to it and started to gobble it up, then went back to playing on Matilda's foot.

"How far is left to go, Oak?"

"Only two miles then we will be there.

We best get on our way, Matilda."

Matilda pulled her feet out of the water and said goodbye to the lake horses. She finished her food and drank the oak cup of water, put her shoes and socks on and walked on.

Oak and Matilda finally reached Ice-cream Mountain.

"We are here," said Oak.

"Brr, its getting cold," said Matilda. She pulled out the coat and hat and put them on. She looked up. It looked like an upside down ice-cream cone.

"I am afraid my journey stops here, Matilda, as Elflings are not allowed up Ice-cream Mountain unless invited by the giants themselves. I will be waiting for your return, do you have your map?"

"Yes." Matilda unrolled the map and put a stone on each end.

"Matilda, you are here. If you follow the twirly path till you get to Turtlegreek, then follow that path to Frightful Freddie's cave. Good luck, Matilda, may the Guardians of Old Magic Prague be with you."

Matilda hugged Oak and set off up the twirly path of Ice-cream Mountain.

Brr, it is getting really cold, thought Matilda to herself, walking up the twirly path and stepping around big boulders. "I hope no rocks fall on my head," she said, looking up. She hugged herself to keep warm. Suddenly, one massive pink snowflake fell by Matilda's feet. "Look at the size of that! It's the size of a Frisbee." Matilda bent down and touched it, it smells of strawberry. She put some in her mouth. *Hmm, it tastes like strawberry ice pop, how lovely.* Another snowflake fell, this one was blue. She ran over to it, *this one smells of blueberry.* She popped a bit in her mouth. *Yum, how exciting, the snowflakes have different flavours.* More snowflakes starting falling: orange, purple, yellow, green, all with their unique flavours, even a white one whose flavour was mint. Matilda started to get a brain freeze. *Ahh! Better get a move on or Oak will be getting worried.*

The higher Matilda climbed, the hotter it became. Wow, it's getting so hot! She took off her jacket and hat and put them back into her satchel. As she just turned the corner, she saw an old wooden sign: "Turtlegreek," and an entrance to a cave. The two turtles were walking side by side, talking to each other, one with a purple shell and the other with a blue one.

"Hello," said Matilda.

They both turned their heads.

"Sorry, we can't stop. We are in a race with each other."

"Who is winning?" asked Matilda.

"Well, it's a draw at the moment."

"Oh, I see."

"We have been racing for one week," said the turtle with the purple shell.

"Wow, one week. Where did you race from?"

"You see that tree, the one that is two steps ahead of you?"

"Yes," said Matilda.

"From there."

"Where does the race finish?"

"To that rock," the turtle will the blue shell said.

"That is fifty yards away and it's taken you a week to get to here?"

"Yes," said the purple-shelled turtle. "I know what you're thinking: its fast, isn't it? They don't call us racer turtles for no reason."

"Indeed," smiled Matilda. "Well, good luck to both of you in your race."

The turtles turned back around, slowly making their way to the rock. Matilda walked into the cave at the side of Ice-cream Mountain. There was massive fire, burning torches on each side of the cave lighting up the way. Matilda suddenly heard a loud whimpering sound.

"Sounds like someone is crying," said Matilda to herself. Matilda made her way through the fire-lit cave till she got to a massive opening. Right in the middle of the cave was a beautiful waterfall and Matilda could not believe it, there was a beach with palm trees with about eight hammocks hanging off each tree and different-coloured coconuts, green seagulls and pink and orange elephants playing in the waterfalls. It was like a paradise island, well, a paradise cave.

"Ow, sob, sob." Matilda heard the crying again. It was coming from the corner. She took a big gulp and walked over to where the crying was. It was Frightful Freddie! He really was a giant. He had purple hair, wore stripy multi-coloured trousers with a big leather belt with a leather bag attached to it, and a pink old-fashioned shirt. He had his back turned away and was holding his foot, sobbing.

Matilda took a deep breath. She was feeling very scared but she knew in her heart that she had to get the magic puppet strings back.

"EXCUSE ME, are you OK?"

Frightful Freddie suddenly turned round angrily.

"Who disturbs me?"

"Er, um, me," said Matilda in a squeaky voice. The giant looked down.

"And who are you?"

"I am Matilda Marsh. Nice to meet you." The giant looked at Matilda for a minute and then said, "I am Freddie, now get out of my cave before I eat you!" He then turned back around. Matilda went bright red with anger.

"Freddie, that wasn't very nice to speak to me like that. No wonder they call you 'Frightful Freddie.' You are very mean." Suddenly, Freddie started crying. His tears fell like pools of water to the floor.

"I am sorry, Matilda, I haven't spoken to anyone in such a long time and my foot is in such pain."

"Well, that's quite alright, Freddie. Now, what's wrong with your foot?

"I have an arrow in it and I can't reach it to get it out. It's so painful."

"OK, maybe I can help you. Let me see your foot." Freddie turned around and stretched out his legs. Matilda walked back and looked at his foot.

"Hmm, I can see the arrow sticking out, your foot looks infected. Freddie, if you can lift me onto that rock, I can pull it out." Freddie picked up Matilda and placed her on the rock. She reached up and quickly pulled the arrow out.

Freddie let out a scream. Matilda rolled her eyes. "Freddie, stop being a drama queen."

"Well, it hurt," said Freddie moodily. Matilda remembered she had cornflowers in her satchel. She pulled them out.

"What is that in your hand?"

"These are cornflowers. It will help with inflammation and it's antiseptic which will heal your infection." Matilda crushed the flower leaves and placed them on the infected area. "Do you have a handkerchief Freddie? Yes, you can wrap it round your foot to keep the leaves in place, take it off in two hours."

"It feels better already, thank you for your kindness, Matilda."

"You're welcome, Freddie. How come you ended up with an arrow in your foot?"

"The Guardian of Protection shot me with it in Old Magic Prague town. You see, Matilda, I get lonely up here on my own."

"Where are the other giants?" said Matilda.

"Well," said Freddie, "they moved up higher on Ice-cream Mountain because they think I am strange because I want to be friends with Elflings. They say giants should be friends with only giants but I don't want to be friends with just giants, I want lots of different friends. So in the end they left me and moved and told me not to follow them until I said I just wanted to be friends with giants. I always hear laughter coming from Old Magic Prague town and they sound like they have so much fun all the time but I have always been scared to go down there in case they don't like me. Being a giant is hard, everybody thinks you are going to eat them and they run away from you because you look scary or different to how they look. They judge you before even getting to know you, and if they took the time to know you, they would find out that all giants are vegetarians."

"So, you don't eat people or Elflings?" said Matilda.

"Ew no, just plants and fruit. I plucked up the courage one day to go down in to the town

and when I arrived, Elflings screamed and ran away and said hurtful things to me like 'please don't eat my children', and then the Guardian of Protection fired his arrow at me. I was so upset that I stole all the magic strings so they couldn't have fun anymore and wept all the way home back to Ice-cream Mountain."

"That is so sad, Freddie, I had no idea. I can see why you took the strings but the Elflings are getting sadder every day and I am sure if I tell them the whole story, they will be very sorry and will invite you to puppet shows more often and not be so scared of you."

"Do you really think they will be my friends?"

"Of course, Freddie. You are the kindest giant I have ever met, well, the only one."

"Well, thank you, Matilda. It's so nice to have someone to talk to." Freddie opened his pouch and handed Matilda the magic strings. She put them in her satchel.

"I better go, Freddie."

"Oh, that's very sad."

"Don't be sad, Freddie, friends always stay in each other's hearts no matter how far the distance."

"We are friends?" said Freddie.

"Of course," said Matilda. "Always. When I get back, I shall speak to Mr Hobbles. Is it OK if he comes and visits you and sorts this terrible mess out?"

"Yes, he can come. I will invite him to Ice-cream Mountain." Freddie reached into his pouch and pulled out some gold glitter dust. He sprinkled it on the ground. Two small gold coins appeared. "Now these coins are special. If a giant catches you on Ice-cream Mountain without an invite, he can throw you off without getting into trouble, but if you show him this coin he can't do anything to you, he has to let you pass,"

Matilda picked one up. It said: "You're invited to Ice-cream Mountain."

"That's the official invite," smiled Freddie. Matilda picked up the other gold coin and it said, "Lifetime invite to Ice-cream Mountain."

"And that coin is for you Matilda, you are always welcome here."

"That is so kind of you, Freddie, thank you." Matilda put the coins in her pocket. "Now, make sure you rest your foot."

"I will, don't worry, Matilda." Matilda shook the giant's hand.

"Take care, Freddie."

"Bye, Matilda."

Matilda headed out the cave door. She saw the turtles again. They had moved about an inch from the last time she saw them.

"You, slow down now guys, I don't want you to injure yourselves!" giggled Matilda.

"No chance of that. We are racing turtles," said the blue turtle. Matilda giggled again and walked back down the twirly path. *Brrr,* it's starting to get cold again. Matilda put her coat and hat back on. The massive snowflakes started to fall again. Matilda waited for a pink one to fall: strawberry was her favourite flavour. She then made it into a snowball and started to eat it while walking back down the mountain.

She reached the bottom of the mountain and Oak jumped up and gave her a massive hug.

"You didn't get eaten by Frightful Freddie. What happened?" asked Oak.

"I will explain everything later, Oak, when we get back to your treehouse."

"Of course," said Oak. "You must be tired." They made their way back through the multi-coloured forest laughing and joking, both of them really happy. They made it to Oak's treehouse and climbed the ladder.

Matilda sat at Oak's table and explained everything that had happened up at Ice cream Mountain while eating slices of applejack. Oak stared in amazement.

"I had no idea poor Frightful... I mean Freddie... I feel so bad and who knew they were vegetarians?"

"I know," said Matilda. "I was amazed too and Freddie was sweet and kind." Matilda showed Oak the gold coins.

"Wow, no Elflings have ever been invited to Ice cream Mountain. This is the biggest thing to have ever happened in Old Magic Prague. I must bubble burp Mr Hobbles and tell him."

Matilda yawned.

"I am off to bed, Oak, I am really tired."

"I bet you are, Matilda. You have travelled far. Good night."

Matilda took off her jacket, hat and shoes as she climbed into the hammock. She pulled the patchwork blanket over her and fell straight to sleep.

Just before the sun rose, Matilda and Oak were making their way back to Old Magic Prague.

"I slept so well, Oak. Your hammocks are so comfy."

"They are, aren't they? Maybe that's why you snore so loud Matilda."

"I don't snore."

"Yes, you do. You sound like a broken down train."

"No, I don't." Oak started laughing. Matilda started chasing him.

"I am only joking," laughed Oak. "You don't really snore."

"I know, I don't snore," giggled Matilda. Matilda then hid behind a massive leaf. Oak stopped running and turned around.

"Matilda, where are you?" Oak walked back and then suddenly, Matilda jumped out from behind the massive leaf and yelled, "Got ya!" Oak screamed then laughed and chased Matilda. Oak and Matilda had fun and laughter all the way back to Old Magic Prague. They reached the big pond. Tony the Toad stood up on the lily pad and started clapping.

"The heroes return! Well done, you must hurry now. Mr Hobbles and the town are waiting for you two now."

"OK," they both said together. They walked down the path into town. All the Elflings were out in the town centre and as soon as they saw them, the Elflings started clapping, cheering, whistling, patting their backs, giving them flowers and throwing rose petals over their heads. Oak and Matilda held hands through the cheers. Mr Hobbles suddenly appeared.

"Welcome back you two!" and gave them both a massive hug. Mr Hobbles banged his stick on the floor.

"Quiet please, hush now." The Elflings went quiet. "I would like to say a few words. First of all, I would like to thank Matilda for her courage, and Oak for his dedication in helping Matilda. Without these two, Old Magic Prague would be a very sad and dark place. I would like this day to be a national holiday. We shall celebrate this day every year with a feast. We shall call the holiday M.O. Day to celebrate Matilda's and Oak's journey. Now, Matilda, if you would please hand over the magic strings." Matilda pulled the magic strings out her bag and gave them to Mr Hobbles, Mr Hobbles threw them in the air and the strings vanished. Suddenly, the wooden puppets started to move and dance. The Elflings began to cheer again and dance and drink applejack cider.

Mr Hobbles took Matilda back to his bookshop, Mr Hobbles opened the blue door and they both walked in.

"Matilda, my girl, you did it!"

"I have something for you, Mr Hobbles." She handed him the gold coin and explained everything in detail about what had happened on Ice cream Mountain.

"I have been a foolish old man. It says in the books that giants eat people. I suppose books can even be wrong sometimes. I had no idea that they are vegetarians, how extraordinary. I shall hold a town meeting tomorrow and explain everything to the Elflings and then visit Freddie and apologise and tell him he can come down anytime. I may be wise, Matilda, but I don't know everything. Thank you for your help. Now go and enjoy the festivities, my girl. You deserve them."

Matilda made her way out the bookshop and joined the party. The Elfling band was playing. Oak grabbed her and they started dancing, swinging each other around, clapping, drinking applejack cider and watching the wooden puppets do a show, which was really funny. Suddenly, Matilda caught something glittering in the corner of her eye by the bookshop. She made her way through the crowd and there it was in all its glory—the magic bike.

It had appeared again suddenly. Mr Hobbles walked behind her.

"It is time, Matilda," he said softly.

"I know Mr Hobbles," she hugged him good bye and Oak walked over. He saw the bike. His faced dropped.

"I suppose you will be off then back to the human world." Matilda nodded. "I will miss you, Matilda."

"I will miss you too." Oak handed Matilda a necklace.

"That is beautiful, Oak. What is it made from?"

"Applejack stalks, I made it for you. When you were at Ice cream Mountain." Matilda put the necklace on and hugged Oak.

"You take care now, Matilda."

"I will never forget you," Matilda said with tears in her eyes.

"And we will always remember you," said Mr Hobbles. Matilda got on the bike, waved and started peddling. Sparks started to fly everywhere and the noises began. The bike started to twirl around. Matilda held on really tight again and closed her eyes.

"Here we go," she screamed as the bike started spinning around. Suddenly the bike stopped.

Matilda opened her eyes and very shakily got off the bike and then bang! The bike vanished again, leaving a cloud of smoke this time. Matilda stood in the cellar a while collecting her thoughts.

It did happen. I wasn't dreaming. She touched her applejack stalk necklace. Suddenly, she heard Mr Dudley's footsteps on the stone steps.

"Matilda, are you finished yet? It's getting late."

Oh no, I haven't even started! Mr Dudley will be wondering what I have been doing all day. Hang on, all the clothes are sorted. How on earth is that possible?

"Well done, Matilda. You have been busy."

"Er yes," said Matilda in a puzzled voice.

"You OK, Matilda? You look a bit peaky."

"I am good, Mr Dudley, just a bit tired."

"I bet you are after your hard work. Brilliant, now here is five pounds."

"Mr Dudley, no, that's alright, I didn't really do much."

"Nonsense, Matilda. Look at this place, it looks great." Mr Dudley put the five pounds in Matilda's pocket. "Now on your way. Your grandma will be having your tea ready."

"Thanks, Mr Dudley, bye."

"Bye, Matilda."

Matilda walked outside the shop and bumped into Jessie, Jane, and Jenny.

"Oh, look girls," said Jessie. "It's little orphan Annie. Jane and Jenny started sniggering. Matilda started laughing. "What's so funny Matilda?"

"You three, that's what's funny."

With that Matilda turned around and walked home. Jessie and Jane and Jenny just looked at Matilda looking really puzzled.

Matilda worked the whole summer at Mr Dudley's shop but the bike never appeared again down the cellar. And every day she thought of Oak and the Elflings and hoped one day she would see them again. Matilda had earned enough money to buy her own bike, *one that didn't disappear,* she laughed to herself. Well, the summer was over, back to school.

It was Monday morning, Matilda was putting on her school uniform and combing her hair. Her grandma was shouting for Matilda to hurry up and that her breakfast was ready.

"I will be down in a minute," said Matilda. Matilda tucked her applejack core necklace under her school shirt so one could see it. She made her way downstairs to the kitchen table. Matilda started eating her porridge and banana.

"Oh, Matilda dear, before I forget, I was doing your washing and I found this gold coin in your pocket." Grandma handed it to Matilda.

"I totally forgot about this coin."

"Where did you get it, dear?"

"From a giant, Grandma." Matilda's grandma laughed.

"Such an imagination, Matilda. Now dear, you are riding on your new bike to school?"

"Yes," said Matilda.

"Good, I have to leave now, as I am meeting Mrs Bumble for a meeting about the Long Ashton newsletter. Will you be OK?

"Yes, Grandma, I will be fine."

"OK then, give me a kiss and have a good first day at school."

"Bye, grandma."

"Bye, dear."

Matilda finished her breakfast, put on her raincoat, picked up her school bag and made her way outside to her new bike. *Oh no, it's got a flat tyre! What rotten luck. And I don't have a puncture kit. Well, I suppose I will have to walk.* Matilda started walking to school mumbling about her flat tyre to herself. She wasn't in the best of moods. As she was walking through the forest as a short cut, something caught her eye.

No, it couldn't be, no! By the bush, the magic bike was there, glittering away, beautiful as ever. Matilda had the biggest smile on her face. She ran over and sat on the bike, and kicked up the stand. "I can't wait to see Oak," she said to herself. She started peddling and the sparks started flying. She closed her eyes and the bike started spinning fast again. She held on tight. Suddenly, the bike banged on the floor. She opened her eyes and squeezed the brakes and the bike stopped. She opened her eyes, coughing, as sand was everywhere. *Hang on a minute, this isn't Old Magic Prague. It looks like, no it couldn't be, it is, I am in Egypt.* Matilda looked up, and there in front of her was a massive pyramid.

This is going to be interesting, she thought.

THE END